FEATHER
TALES

D0482556

Blackie Crow

David M. Sargent, Jr., and his friends live in Northwest Arkansas. His writing career began in 1995 with a cruel joke being played on his mother. The friends pictured with him are (from left to right), Vera, Buffy, and Mary.

Dave Sargent is a lifelong resident of the small town of Prairie Grove, Arkansas. A fourth-generation dairy farmer, Dave began writing in early December, 1990. He enjoys the outdoors and has a real love for birds and animals.

Blackie Crow

By

Dave Sargent

Illustrated by
Jane Lenoir

Ozark Publishing, Inc.
P.O. Box 228
Prairie Grove, AR 72753

Library of Congress cataloging-in-publication data

Sargent, Dave, 1941—
    / by Dave and Pat Sargent ; illustrated by Jane Lenoir.
        p. cm.
        Summary: Blackie Crow teaches Satan the Bull that lying is not good and can spoil the fun for everyone. Includes nonfiction information on crows.
        ISBN 1-56763-443-5 (cb). — ISBN 1-56763-444-3 (pb)
        II. Lenoir, Jane,
        —   ill.   III. Title.
                                        CIP
                                                AC

Printed in the United States of America

iv

Inspired by

the many crows who live on our farm.

Dedicated to

all students who love birds--whether they are big or small, good or bad.

Foreword

Blackie the Crow teaches ole Satan the Bull that lying is not good. When you lie, it can spoil all the fun for everyone.

Contents

Blackie Crow

If you would like to have an author of The Feather Tale Series visit your school, free of charge, just call 1-800-321-5671 or 1-800-960-3876.

One

Blackie and the Bovine

The setting sun cast light upon the distant clouds, creating bright shades of lavender, pink, and gold throughout the sky. The barnyard was settling down for a peaceful night of sleep as Blackie the Crow landed on the limb of a tree near the chicken house. This looks perfect, he thought. It's been a good day, and now I'm ready for a good night's sleep! Blackie ruffled his feathers and yawned.

Suddenly he overheard whispers among the animals and birds.

"Did you hear that Farmer John and Molly are having a family reunion here tomorrow?" a voice asked.

"Wow, that's a little scary!" another exclaimed.

"Why is it scary?" the first voice inquired. "And what is a reunion anyway?"

"A reunion is a whole bunch of people getting together to make life miserable for us," a deep, grumpy voice mumbled.

"That doesn't sound so bad," another commented. "As a matter of fact, I think it'll be fun!"

"Fun? Fun?" the grouchy voice responded. "The big people will run over you, the little people will throw rocks at you, and you say it will be fun? Bah, humbug!"

Blackie cocked his head from side to side, trying to spot the fault-finder.

"This is a lot of nonsense," Blackie grumbled. "That fellow is going to frighten the life out of everyone. I better stop the rumors right now or nobody will get any sleep tonight."

Blackie Crow hopped down to a lower branch.

"None of you are safe," the gruff voice continued. "By this time tomorrow, the barnyard will be full of nothing but bruised bodies and bent feathers."

Well, that did it! Blackie Crow hopped to the ground. This kind of talk, he thought, causes big problems, and none of it is true! The gruff voice droned on and on about the upcoming horrible day as Blackie hurried toward the "Oh no's" and "Yipe's" of the fear-riddled audience.

Moments later, the upset crow landed on the corral fence and looked down at Satan the Bull. The bovine was standing right in the middle of the corral, surrounded by frightened residents of Farmer John's place. It was way past bedtime for most of the animals, but they were not moving. Instead they listened, wide-eyed and scared stiff, to every word spoken by Satan, the teller of untrue tales.

"This calls for both drastic and immediate action," Blackie muttered.

The black bird flew from the fence and landed on the back of the bull. He puffed out his chest and straightened his back, hoping to appear bigger and more commanding in appearance. Blackie cleared his throat as he looked down at each member of the audience.

"Don't listen to him," Blackie

said in a very loud voice. "He is not telling you the truth! Tomorrow will be a day of fun and games. This old bull lies when the truth fits better."

Blackie Crow again looked at the spectators. He remained silent as they whispered and mumbled among themselves. Satan the Bull shuffled his hooves and strained to see who dared to defy his word. He snorted and pawed the ground, but Blackie did not leave. That little crow was determined to stop the rising panic.

"Farmer John is our friend," Blackie shouted, "and the people coming tomorrow are his relatives and friends. They will not run over us or throw rocks at us."

Blackie hopped to the ground and glared up at ole Satan the Bull.

"You, Sir, are a troublemaker and a fibber!" he declared.

Satan pawed the ground and bellowed angrily. Seconds later, he charged at Blackie, but the crow hopped to one side.

As the bovine turned to charge again, the farm animals scattered into the shadows of evening, and only Satan and Blackie remained in the corral.

"There is no one left to listen to you," Blackie declared. "Now go to bed. Forget about spreading any more vicious lies!" Blackie yawned before adding, "Now, I'm tired, and I'm going to bed. I suggest you do the same. Good night!"

Without further comment, he flew to the tree beside the chicken house and, mere moments later, was snoring softly.

Two

The Troublemaker

The eastern horizon was filling with light as Blackie awoke and stretched his wings. He ruffled his feathers and looked around the barnyard. The air seemed filled with excitement and a bit of apprehension. He flew to the trouble spot of the previous night and landed on the corral fence. A small group of nervous animals was again gathered, listening to Satan the Bull.

"Just remember," the big bull whispered, "stay out of sight today or

the big people will run over you, and
the little people will throw rocks at
you." The big bull shook his head
sadly before adding, "By nightfall
there will be nothing left but bruised
bodies and bent feathers."

Blackie Crow hopped down
from the fence. He beat his wings on
the ground and jumped up and down
in a frenzied fit.

"I told you he is lying!" Blackie screamed. "Don't listen to him. Farmer John would not bring folks here to hurt you!"

This fit continued for several minutes before Blackie realized that he and Satan the Bull were the lone occupants of the corral. He glared at Satan.

"You tell lies that hurt and frighten others," Blackie panted. "What are you going to say when they find out that you lied?"

"Oh, they'll all be hiding," the big Jersey bull chuckled. "They'll never know the truth."

The conversation was suddenly cut short by the sound of vehicles arriving. Farmer John and Molly were laughing and greeting guests as they carried food into the house.

"Anyone who wants to meet the animals," Farmer John said proudly, "follow me. We have some special friends in the barnyard, and I know they're anxious to meet you."

Frightened little eyes peered from behind rocks, fence posts, and buildings as Farmer John led people, big and little, toward the barn.

"Hmmm," Farmer John said to Molly. "Something must be terribly wrong!"

Molly pointed toward a band of sheep that were huddled in a corner of the pasture. They were trembling. The horse, mule, and some cows were crowded into another corner. They were staring, wide-eyed and frightened, at everyone. Farmer John reached the chicken pen, and all the chickens squawked and ran into the chicken house. The pigs squealed and ran behind their wooden shed.

Farmer John looked at Molly. A tear was streaming down her cheek.

"Our animals are sick, John," she said. "We must postpone the reunion and phone the veterinarian."

"You're right," Farmer John agreed. "Everyone's been looking forward to being with our animals. Why, these folks even brought special treats for them." Farmer John shook his head sadly. "But they can't enjoy treats if they're sick."

Farmer John, Molly, and their guests went back toward the house.

Blackie sat on the corral fence near ole Satan, the mean Jersey bull, watching and listening to the awful consequences of the lies.

"Well, are you satisfied, Satan?" Blackie Crow scolded. "See what you've done? You have completely ruined the family reunion, and you have disappointed all of the guests. And," he shouted, "you have cost all the animals a special day of treats!"

Satan the Bull looked down at the ground. He shuffled his hooves in the dirt.

"I feel real bad about making Molly cry," he groaned. "And now Farmer John is going to call the vet. Oh, woe is me, Blackie Crow, what can I do to make everything all right again?"

"Well," Blackie Crow said, "for starters you might tell the animals the truth." Blackie cocked his head to one side and paused for a moment before adding, "And if you are sincere about correcting your fibs, I think I know a solution. Now, listen carefully, Satan.

By speaking the truth and working together, we can . . ."

Three

Never Tell a Lie

Minutes later, the animals were once again grouped around ole Satan. Blackie Crow sat upon his back as Satan apologized and told them of his bad deed.

"I didn't mean to hurt anybody," Satan mumbled. "I was just having fun scaring you."

Blackie whispered, "Don't forget to . . ."

"Yes. I know, Blackie," the bull agreed quietly. "I'm coming to that." He cleared his throat and, in a loud clear voice said, "But one should never tell a lie. Even if it seems harmless and fun."

Blackie smiled as he watched the barnyard animals begin to relax.

"We must stop Farmer John," the black crow said. "And you must be ready to meet and greet the nice folks."

"This will be fun!" an excited voice exclaimed.

"Yes, fun!" the others agreed in unison.

"Okay, Satan Bull," Blackie said. "You know what to do. Go for it!"

The bull bellowed and pawed the ground. He bucked and bawled before blasting his way through the corral fence. Then the barnyard menagerie followed Satan as he ran toward the house at full speed. He veered to the left as Farmer John opened the door. The man had a bewildered look on his face, but he smiled as he watched all the animals line up to greet his guests.

"Molly!" he shouted. "Everybody come here!"

Only seconds later, everyone was in the front yard. Their smiles welcomed the animals, and their treats sealed a lasting friendship. A young boy ran toward Satan the Bull. His eyes sparkled with admiration.

"Look, Mama!" he shouted. "Isn't the bull magnificent?"

The afternoon hours were filled with fun and games and plenty to eat. The big people showered the livestock with praise, while the little people included them in their games of tag, softball, and frisbee.

That evening Blackie found Satan the Bull standing in a corner with his head bowed.

"Are you okay?" Blackie asked. "Didn't you enjoy the reunion?"

"Oh yes, I did," Satan Bull said quietly. "I enjoyed the treats and the games and the people very much."

"Why are you looking so sad then?" the crow inquired. "It sounds like you had a great day, and that boy even said you are magnificent. Why, that should make you very happy and very, very proud!"

"I'm not magnificent," the bull groaned. "I am a liar--and a fibber. I almost ruined the reunion for everybody!"

Blackie Crow shook his head. "Shame on you, Satan Bull. You are not a liar."

Satan glared at Blackie Crow. "I am, too!"

"No you aren't, Satan," the crow insisted. "You lied in the past, but you do not intend to do it again, do you?"

"No!" the bull bellowed. "I will never tell a lie again, Blackie Crow! I promise!"

Blackie the Crow smiled and nodded his head. "You see, Satan?" Blackie said smugly. "You're not a liar! Now I'm very tired, and I'm going to bed. Good night, my friend."

Satan the Bull smiled and said, "Good night, my friend."

Blackie Crow flew to the big oak tree beside the chicken house. He landed on a limb and yawned. It's been a good day, he thought as he ruffled his feathers and sat down. I wonder what tomorrow will bring. Hmmm . . .

Four

Crow Facts

Crow (bird), is a common name for about 27 large passerine birds of the genus which also includes the ravens and jackdaws. Their family also includes the jays, magpies, choughs, and nutcrackers. Crows are found on every continent except South America and Antarctica. They are among the most intelligent and adaptable of birds, and several species have been able to thrive near humans, although others, especially on islands, are endangered and their habits little known. Northern-hemisphere crows are sometimes migratory, but often they are resident the year round. Although territorial in the breeding season, crows are gregarious at other times, and wintering flocks may number in the thousands.

In the breeding season, crows gather together to mob owls and other predators. Crows in turn may be mobbed by other birds, because their omnivorous diet includes eggs and nestlings as well as other small animals, vegetable matter, carrion, and garbage.

In some agricultural areas, crows are considered great pests, which accounts for the invention of the scarecrow. Crow nests are large platforms of sticks, usually in tall trees. The three to eight eggs are deeply colored and are incubated by the female. The young are cared for by both parents. The voices of crows are loud and usually harsh, but are characteristic for each species.

All of the North American crows are black, with more or less of a glossy sheen, but several species from elsewhere are conspicuously marked with white or gray. The best known species is the ubiquitous American crow, which has become increasingly adapted to urban areas in the late 20th century. It is up to 20 inches long. A similar species, differing in voice, is the northwestern crow, confined to the Pacific coast from Alaska to Oregon.

A smaller, glossier species, the fish crow, lives along the Atlantic and Gulf coasts from New England to Texas and inland along major river systems. The tiny Mexican crow, also known as the Tamaolipas crow, is regularly seen in southeastern Texas.

Classifications: Crows belong to the family *Corvidae* of the order *Passeriformes.* The American crow is classified as *Corvus brachyrhynchos*, the northwestern crow as *Corvus caurinus*, the fish crow as *Corvus ossifragus*, and the Mexican crow as *Corvus imparatus*.